Epaminondas

Epam

Illustrated by Trina Schart Hyman

inondas

RETOLD BY Eve Merriam

Follett Publishing Company

Chicago Ⓕ *New York*

LIBRARY OF CONGRESS CATALOG CARD NUMBER: 68-10476

First Printing

Follett Publishing Company
1010 West Washington Boulevard
Chicago, Illinois 60607

T/L 2224

Adapted from *Epaminondas and His Auntie* in
Stories to Tell to Children by Sara Cone Bryant,
with permission of Houghton Mifflin Company.

For Diana

Epaminondas and his mother lived on one side of the hill. His grandmother and grandfather lived on the other side of the hill.

Whenever Epaminondas went to visit his grandparents, they gave him something to take home.

7

One day his grandmother gave him a
big piece of cake that she had just baked.
It was rich and yellow and round as the
sun in the sky. It was still warm from the
oven, and the smell was so delicious that
Epaminondas could feel his toes turning up.

"I'll be careful with it," Epaminondas
said to his granny. "I won't drop a crumb
of it on the way home."

8

He held the cake tightly in his fist and walked down the hill carefully. He was careful not to trip on any pebbles along the way. And he headed straight home. He didn't even stop to watch the fish waggling in the brook. Or listen to the birds jabbering in the trees. He didn't whittle himself a stick. He went straight home.

By the time he got home, all he had was a fistful of crumbs.

"What do you have there, Epaminondas?" asked his mother.

"Cake, Mama," said Epaminondas.

"Cake!" said his mother, as she tweaked his ear. "Epaminondas, sometimes I think you haven't even got the sense you were born with. That's not the way to carry cake. The way to carry cake is to wrap it all up in leaves and put it in your hat and then put your hat on your head and come along home. Now, will you remember that?"

"Yes, Mama," said Epaminondas.

The next week Epaminondas went to visit his grandparents again. This time they gave him a pound of fresh butter to take home. It had just been churned and it was cool and pale as moonlight and there were drops of moisture on it that sparkled like dew. That fresh butter certainly would taste good on some bread when he got home. And he'd be hungry after the walk.

He waved good-bye and started off
with the butter. He remembered exactly
what his mother had told him. He wrapped
the butter in leaves and put it in his hat
and then put his hat on his head and came
along home.

Soon the sun began to shine brightly. It shone down on the trees and down on the bushes and down on Epaminondas' hat. Epaminondas began to feel warmer and warmer. Pale, shiny drops ran down his forehead, matted his eyebrows, stuck to his eyelashes. He sniffed, and drops of butter sniffled into his nose. The drops clung to his chin and trickled on down his neck, inside his collar, and under his shirt. The butter kept on running down, down, all the way to the undersides of his feet. Still he kept on walking with his head held high and his hat on his head all the way home.

When he got home, all the butter Epaminondas had was *on him.*

His mother looked at him, and she cried out, "Epaminondas, what do you have in your hat?"

"Butter, Mama," said Epaminondas, "Grandma and Grandpa gave it to me."

"Butter!" exclaimed his mother as she tweaked his ear. "Epaminondas, sometimes I know you haven't even got the sense you were born with. That's not the way to carry butter. The way to carry butter is to wrap it up in leaves, then take it down to the brook and cool it in the water and cool it in the water and cool it in the water. Then take it carefully in your hands and come along home. Now, will you remember that?"

"Yes, Mama," said Epaminondas, "I'll remember. I'll remember."

After a while, Epaminondas went to visit his grandparents again, and they gave him a frisky little puppy-dog to take home. The puppy-dog yipped and yapped and flipped its stubby tail and flapped its floppy ears.

Epaminondas hugged the puppy-dog close to him while he gathered some leaves. He wrapped it up in the leaves and took it down to the brook and cooled it in the water and cooled it in the water and cooled it in the water and then he took it in his hands and came along home.

His mother looked at him and said, "Epaminondas, what do you have there?"

"It's a frisky little puppy-dog," Epaminondas answered. "Only it's not frisky any more. I don't know why. I carried it home carefully, just the way you told me to."

The puppy-dog was whimpering and shaking. "Here," said his mother, "give it here." She rubbed the puppy-dog dry and then tweaked its ears. The puppy gave a yip and a yap and began to wag its stubby tail.

Now his mother shook her head. "Epaminondas," she said, "for sure and certain you haven't got the sense you were born with. The way to carry a puppy-dog is to take a long piece of string and put one end around the dog's neck, not too

tight and not too loose. And then you set the puppy down on the ground very gently. Very, very gently so you don't scare it, and then you tie the other end of the string around your hand and you come along home. Now remember."

"I'll remember, Mama, I'll remember," said Epaminondas.

A few weeks later Epaminondas climbed over the hill to visit his grandmother again. This time his grandmother gave him a loaf of fresh-baked bread to take home. It was beautiful and brown and crusty.

Epaminondas waved good-bye and then took a long piece of string from his pocket. He tied one end around the bread, not too tight and not too loose. Then he set the loaf of bread down on the ground very gently. Very, very gently. And he tied the other end of the string around his hand and walked on home.

When his mother saw him, she took one look at the dusty thing on the end of the string, and she let out a little scream. "Epaminondas, what is that old thing you are dragging in here?"

"Fresh-baked bread, Mama," said Epaminondas. "Grandma sent it to us."

"Bread!!" said his mother. "Epaminondas, you don't have the sense you were born with. Now I am not going to tell you any more ways to carry things home from grandma and grandpa. *I'm* going to see them myself. I'll be back soon, and you be good and careful while I'm gone. Do you hear?"

"I hear, Mama," said Epaminondas.

"Watch out when you go outside to play," his mother said, "I've got six mince pies cooling on the doorstep and *you be careful how you step on those pies!*"

Then Epaminondas' mother filled a basket with good things to eat and went away to see his grandmother and grandfather.

The six mince pies sat cooling in a row on the doorstep.

As soon as his mother left, Epaminondas went out on the porch, and he was good and careful. He stepped—right—in

—the—middle—of—each—one!

When his mother came back she said, "Epaminondas, it's plain to me now. You don't have the sense you were born with. And you never will have the sense you were born with. But I love you just the same, and don't you forget it."

"Don't worry, Mama," said Epaminondas. "I won't forget it."

And he never did.